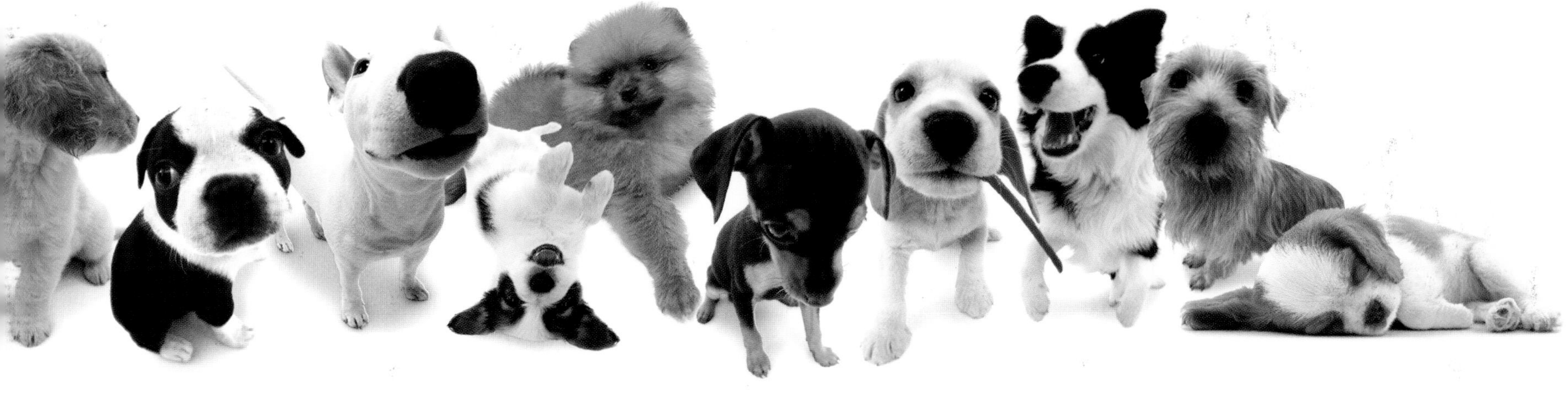

THE DOG

from Arf! Arf!

to Zzzzzz

THE
DOG
Artlist Collection

THE DOG

from

Arf!

Arf!

to

Zzzzzz

HarperCollins*Publishers*

Library of Congress catalog card number: 2003018720

Typography by Martha Rago

1 2 3 4 5 6 7 8 9 10

❖

First Edition

*Dedicated to
the dog lovers
of the world*

A

Arf!
Arf!

B

Beg.

C

Come!

D

Down.

E

Eat

F

Fetch!

G

**Good
dog.**

H

Howwwwl!

Itch,
itch,
itch

J

Jump!

K

Kiss,
kiss

L

Lie down.

M

Mmmmmm

No!

Oops

P

Paw

Q

Quiet.

R

Roll over and over. and over.

S

Sit!
Stay!

T

Tail

U

Upside down

V

Vroom! Vroom!

W

Wag, wag, wag

X

**X marks
the spot.**

Y

Yawn

Zzzzz

Breeds

Front and back cover
Dalmatian

Half-title page
West Highland terrier

Title page
Tibetan spaniel

Copyright page
Golden retriever

A
Bull terrier

B
Jack Russell terrier

C
Labrador retriever

D
Boxer

E
Shih tzu

F
Beagle

G
St. Bernard

H
Newfoundland

I
Shiba

J
Border collie

K
Cocker spaniel

L
Poodle

M
Pug

N
Miniature pinscher

O
Boston terrier

P
Maltese

Q
Welsh corgi

R
Bernese mountain dog

S
Norfolk terrier

T
Dachshund

U
Papillon

V
Papillon

W
Cavalier King Charles spaniel

X
Pomeranian

Y
Miniature schnauzer

Z
Cavalier King Charles spaniel

Opposite page
Papillon